Oct. 6, 2017

To all my friends
at Mrs. Gracia's class
at HFHN School —

Love,
Susanna Bell

For Leo Racine, who I love more than all the fish in all the ponds in all the world!

- Nonni

www.mascotbooks.com

Fishing in the Pond

©2016 Susanna Bell. All Rights Reserved. No part of this publication may be reproduced, stored in a retrieval system or transmitted in any form by any means electronic, mechanical, or photocopying, recording or otherwise without the permission of the author.

For more information, please contact:
Mascot Books
560 Herndon Parkway #120
Herndon, VA 20170
info@mascotbooks.com

Library of Congress Control Number: 2016915449

CPSIA Code: PRT1016A
ISBN-13: 978-1-63177-871-1

Printed in the United States

Fishing
in the
Pond

By
Susanna Bell

Leo was in his favorite spot in the kitchen by the window looking at pictures of fish. Daddy was cooking breakfast on the stove, while Mama put plates on the table.

"What should we do today?" Mama asked.

Leo said, "Let's go fishing."

Mama said, "What about a picnic?"

"But what about fishing? I've never fished before!"

"Let's have a picnic at the park," said Mama. "We can fish there too."

After breakfast, Daddy drove to the pond in the woods. "This looks like a good spot," said Mama as she spread a blanket out on the ground.

"Oh no!" shouted Leo. "We don't have a fishing pole! How can we fish without a fishing pole?"

Daddy smiled as he walked through the woods. Leo chased after him and picked up the first branch he found.

It was so wide he could hardly hold it. Daddy said, "That branch will not do."

A much narrower branch was a few steps away. Leo picked it up off the ground. It was twice as tall as him and waved side to side as he held it over his head.

Mama shook her head. "That branch will not do."

They walked through the woods a little longer.

"How about this one?" asked Leo.

The branch he was holding was making music! There were smaller twigs sprouting from it, and at the end, a little bird was singing a song.

Mama and Daddy said it was a lovely
branch, and the singing bird was nice.

But, as a fishing pole, Daddy said,
"That branch will not do."

Leo was getting discouraged. He thought he would never find a good branch. If he didn't find one, he wouldn't be able to fish today. Then he spotted a branch near his feet.

It was just wide enough to hold in his hands. When he held it up over his head, it was just tall enough not to bend in the wind.

"This branch will do nicely," said Mama.

Daddy wrapped a heavy string around one end of the branch and tied a fish hook at the tip of the string. Mama dug up a worm and placed it across the fish hook.

Leo sat on the bank of the pond with the string hanging the worm in the water below them. He held the branch tightly and watched for a tug.

There was splashing, and the string was being pulled away! Leo held tightly to the pole, and Mama helped him to draw the fish out of the water.

Leo laughed and shouted happily
that he had caught his first fish.
Mama took it off the hook and put it
in a special basket to take home.

But first, Daddy took a picture of Leo
holding the fish.

As they drove home from the pond, Mama asked Leo if he would like to eat his fish for supper.

"What?" asked Leo. "I can't eat my fish! I'm keeping him as a pet!"

So Mama said, "This fish is too big to live in a fishbowl. Fish like these are not meant to be pets."

Leo was sad.

Daddy stopped the car at a pet store, where they let Leo pick out a fishbowl, some fish food, colorful rocks, and a plastic coral reef.

Leo chose a beautiful, little fish to bring home as a pet.

Leo was sitting in the kitchen, in his favorite spot. The **fishbowl** was in front of him, and he was tapping the glass to get his **fish's** attention.

Daddy asked Leo, "What will you name your **fish**?"

"I think I'll call him _____."

Mama was cooking supper, and it smelled
really good.

About the Author

When caring for her first grandchild when he was only a few months old, Susanna Bell told him a story about a little boy who loved fishing. He was so enchanted that he slept through the night for the first time…and that story became *Fishing in the Pond*. Susanna can't wait until Leo is old enough to read it aloud to her.

Susanna is an artist and writer from the south coast of Massachusetts, who considers New Hampshire to be her second home.